It's What's Inside That Counts

written by Shawn A. McMullen
illustrated by Amanda Haley

CIP DATA AVAILABLE
Library of Congress Catalog Card Number 90-71158
Copyright ©1991, The STANDARD PUBLISHING Company, Cincinnati, Ohio.
A division of STANDEX INTERNATIONAL Corporation.
Printed in U.S.A.   24-03898

It was a wonderful morning. The buds on the trees had burst into beautiful new leaves. The wild flowers spread across the meadows like colorful blankets. The birds sang and the sun shone big and bright and yellow. Spring had come to the deep woods. And no one loved spring more than Justin Ordinary Squirrel.

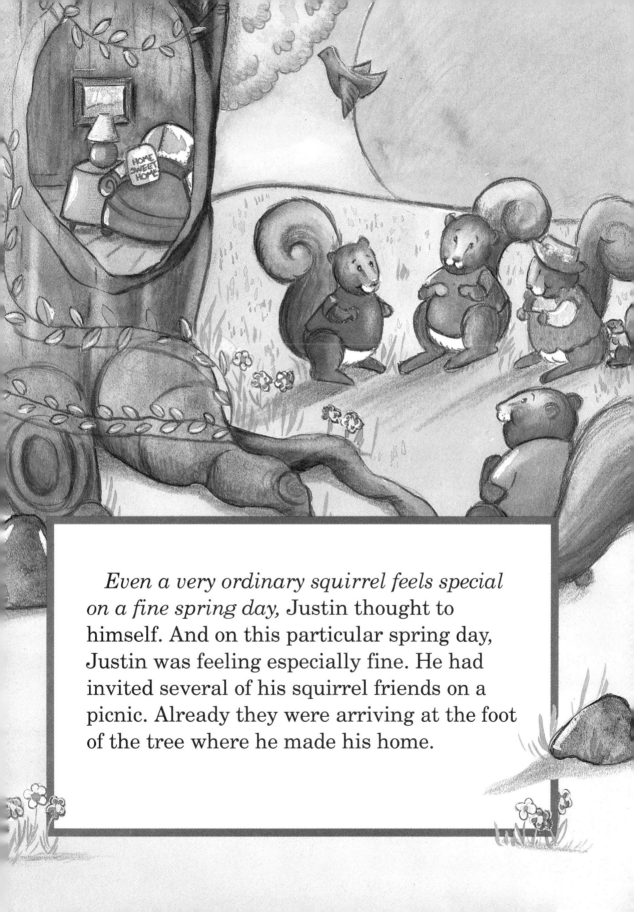

Even a very ordinary squirrel feels special on a fine spring day, Justin thought to himself. And on this particular spring day, Justin was feeling especially fine. He had invited several of his squirrel friends on a picnic. Already they were arriving at the foot of the tree where he made his home.

There was plenty of time before lunch, so Justin suggested a game of hide-and-seek. And since it was Justin's idea, his friends decided that he should be "it" first. So he leaned against a large rock to start counting as his friends hurried to find hiding places.

Suddenly, an unpleasant smell drifted into the woods. Justin and his friends recognized it at once.

"Skunk!" yelled a squirrel who had hidden inside a hollow log. He scrambled out in pretend panic, holding a paw over his nose and running as fast as his other three legs could carry him.

"Polecat! Run for your lives!" shouted another as he climbed a large oak tree and disappeared into its leaves. He tried to sound frightened, but his laughter gave him away.

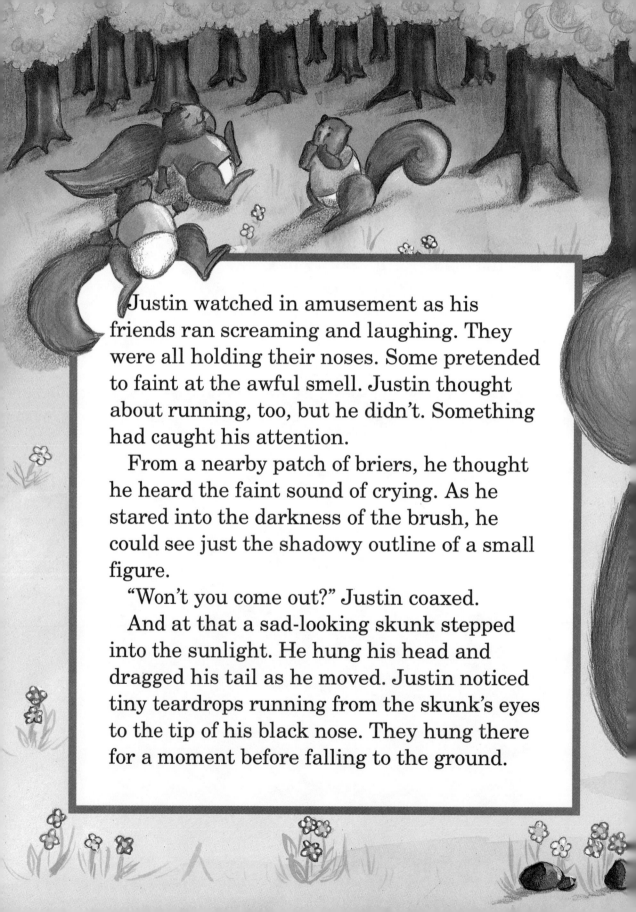

Justin watched in amusement as his friends ran screaming and laughing. They were all holding their noses. Some pretended to faint at the awful smell. Justin thought about running, too, but he didn't. Something had caught his attention.

From a nearby patch of briers, he thought he heard the faint sound of crying. As he stared into the darkness of the brush, he could see just the shadowy outline of a small figure.

"Won't you come out?" Justin coaxed.

And at that a sad-looking skunk stepped into the sunlight. He hung his head and dragged his tail as he moved. Justin noticed tiny teardrops running from the skunk's eyes to the tip of his black nose. They hung there for a moment before falling to the ground.

"Well, aren't you going to make fun of me and run away like the others?" the skunk asked in a tone that was half hurt and half anger.

"No, I don't think I will," replied Justin.

"Why not?"

"Because I think it's mean," Justin responded. "And if I were in your place, I think it would make me feel simply awful."

The skunk nodded in agreement. "You're right about that." He looked up at Justin and continued, "Do you have any idea how hard it is to make friends when you're a skunk?"

"I guess I never thought about it much," Justin confessed.

"Well, I've thought about it a lot," the skunk said, "and it's very hard. I've tried and tried, but every time I get close to other animals they run away. Some, like your friends, even make a game of it, calling me names and holding their noses. I guess it wouldn't be so bad if there were other skunks in this part of the woods. At least then I'd have someone to talk to."

"You must get very lonely," Justin said.
The little skunk blinked several times to hold back the tears. "You know," he continued "it's not my fault I smell this way. I didn't ask to be born a skunk." Then he sighed, "Oh, what's the use talking about it? I may as well accept the fact that I'll never have any friends. Who would want to be friends with a . . . with a . . . skunk?" And with that he slowly turned to walk back into the brier patch.

"W-wait!" stammered Justin nervously. Being a very ordinary squirrel, he was seldom sure of what to say. But he knew what to say at that moment. "I would."

The skunk stopped. "You would what?"

"I would want to be friends with a skunk. I mean, I would like to be your friend."

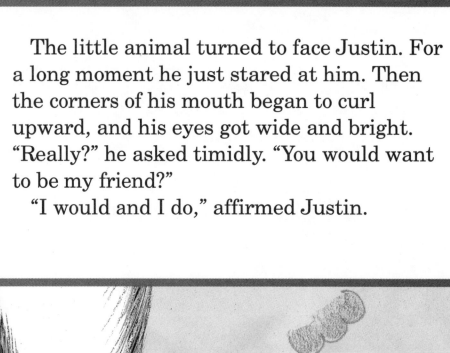

The little animal turned to face Justin. For a long moment he just stared at him. Then the corners of his mouth began to curl upward, and his eyes got wide and bright. "Really?" he asked timidly. "You would want to be my friend?"

"I would and I do," affirmed Justin.

"Oh boy!" shouted the excited skunk as he rushed back to Justin. He talked so quickly Justin could barely understand him. "But I don't even know your name. I must know your name. If we're going to be friends, we really must know each other's name!" He reached out a paw to shake as he said with enthusiasm, "I'm Gregory."

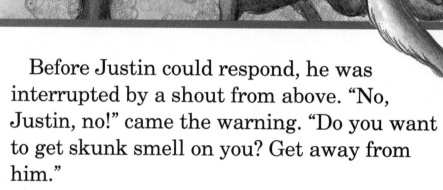

Before Justin could respond, he was interrupted by a shout from above. "No, Justin, no!" came the warning. "Do you want to get skunk smell on you? Get away from him."

Justin looked up. Lying in the branches and clinging to the tree trunks all around him were the squirrel friends he had been playing with. They all began to chatter. "Run, Justin, run! Get away while you still smell like a squirrel!"

Justin glanced back at Gregory. He wasn't smiling anymore. He was slowly pulling back his paw. Justin looked up again at his friends. He paused for an instant, and then he did a very kind and brave thing.

"And I'm Justin," he said warmly. And instead of shaking Gregory's paw, Justin threw open his arms and gave the little skunk a great big hug.

The smile reappeared on Gregory's face. "Then you really do want to be my friend!" he said gratefully. And then he returned Justin's hug.

Justin felt good inside. That is, until he noticed all his squirrel friends leaving. They chattered loudly to one another as they left the woods. Some shook their heads angrily. Justin knew they were upset.

"I'm sorry about your friends," Gregory said sadly as he watched them leave. "I guess it's all my fault."

"Don't worry about it," Justin reassured him. "They're still my friends. They just don't understand yet." And then he smiled at Gregory.

"But enough about that. Are you hungry? We've got a big picnic lunch to eat."

Justin and Gregory spent the rest of that day together. And in the days that followed they became the best of friends. This made Justin very happy. But he was still bothered that his squirrel friends would not accept Gregory. Nothing he could say would convince them to change their minds.

"He's a skunk and we're squirrels," they said whenever Justin brought up the subject. "He's just too different."

"He may be different on the outside, but on the inside he's very kind and wonderful. I'm sure you'd like him if you got to know him."

But still they wouldn't listen. "You'll regret the day you ever made friends with a smelly ol' skunk, Justin!" they warned. Justin could only hope that someday they would see things differently.

The weeks passed, and spring turned to summer. One summer morning Justin awoke to a most unusual feeling. His head ached, his stomach hurt, and he could scarcely get up on all fours. He didn't feel like eating or playing or sleeping. He felt miserable. And as the day wore on, he got worse. He lay in his hole in the tree feeling sick and alone and frightened. *What is happening to me?* he thought.

Just then he heard Gregory's familiar voice. "Hey Justin!" he called from the foot of the tree, "Would you like to go for a walk? It's a beautiful afternoon."

Justin pulled himself to the opening of his
hole and looked down at Gregory. "I wish I
could," he said weakly, "but I feel terrible.
My head aches, my stomach hurts, and I can
barely move. I've been like this all day."

The cheerful expression on Gregory's face gave way to a worried look. "Justin," he demanded, "come down here and let me take a look at you."

"Really, Gregory, I . . ."

"Come down at once!" Gregory said sternly.

Justin had never known Gregory to act this way before, and so, as difficult as it was, he slowly made his way down the tree. Gregory took one look at Justin and said confidently, "Just what I thought. Squirrel fever."

"Squirrel fever?" asked Justin with alarm. "What's that?"

"It's a kind of virus," Gregory explained. "Among squirrels it's quite contagious—and very dangerous."

"Dangerous?" Justin repeated nervously.

"It can be," replied Gregory. "If it isn't treated, it can make you very, very sick—or worse!"

Justin gasped.

"Stay here. I'll be right back," Gregory said as he ran off into the woods. He returned in minutes with a cup filled with a dark, pasty mixture.

"Here. Swallow this," he ordered.

Justin brought the cup to his mouth. "It smells awful," he protested.

"Oh, I hadn't noticed," smiled Gregory. "I guess I don't pay much attention to the way things smell."

"What's in it?" Justin asked.

"Just some herbs and roots and flowers," Gregory replied. "It will make you feel better in a jiffy. Go on, take it."

Justin did. And in no time his pain was gone and he could stand again. He looked at Gregory in amazement. "How did you do that?" he asked.

"Do what?" inquired Gregory.

"You know," Justin said impatiently. "How did you know what plants to mix together to make me well?"

"Oh, I know lots about plants," Gregory said. "My father taught me. We used to gather all different kinds of plants from the woods. Then we dried them and stored them. When anyone around us got sick or hurt, we mixed up something to help him. Once you learn what to mix with what, you can cure almost anything."

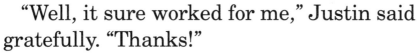

"Well, it sure worked for me," Justin said gratefully. "Thanks!"

"Think nothing of it," said Gregory. "That's what friends are for."

"Friends!" Justin blurted out suddenly. "My squirrel friends! Gregory, did you say this squirrel fever is contagious?"

"Oh yes," Gregory confirmed. "It can be passed on quite easily. Chances are one of your squirrel friends gave it to you."

"Then I've got to check on them," Justin said urgently.

"And I'm going with you," Gregory insisted. "Some of them may be sick and need my medicine, too."

The two set off immediately. They spent the rest of that day and the next two traveling through the woods, checking on all the other squirrels. And some were very sick indeed, much sicker even than Justin had been. But with a cup of Gregory's special mixture, every squirrel was soon up and about, fully recovered.

Not long afterward, Justin and his squirrel friends met for another picnic. And this time the guest of honor was none other than Gregory Skunk himself.

Justin's friends were very apologetic. "Can you ever forgive us for acting so stupidly?" they asked Gregory. "If it weren't for you, we might not even be alive today. We certainly misjudged you, friend."

"And you were right all along," they said to Justin. "You saw something in Gregory none of the rest of us was able to see. We know now that it doesn't matter what's on the outside, it's what's on the inside that really counts."

Gregory smiled.

"I'm just glad we're all friends now," said a very happy Justin, "so let's finish that game of hide-and-seek!"

And they did.

"People look at the outside of a person, but the Lord looks at the heart" (1 Samuel 16:7, ICB).